To Garrett, thanks for inspiring this story!
Love you!

How It All Began

I love my blue truck;
I'm sure you can see.
It has been my favorite
since I was three!

It's been a real good truck;
it has lasted through the years

Up until just recently,
when it started
missing gears.

I'll admit it has its flaws, that blue beast I call my truck. Its wheels are getting slick, and the shifter keeps getting stuck!

And just yesterday, the sadness sure set in. It was finally stuck for good; reverse was all it did.

At first, I was heartbroken; I thought, *I'm really out of luck. How can I survive out in the country without my favorite pickup truck?*

Well, since my truck got stuck in reverse,
I've had lots of time to practice.
My driving skills had much improved; I
really got good at going backward!

One day, my pal, my very best friend, my cousin he is, you see. He said, "I bet you can't reverse that thing through them yonder trees!"

I took the bet; I knew I'd win and show him I was the best. After seeing my skills, he'd have to say, "You really are better than all the rest!"

I checked the battery; it was good, and
I checked everything under the hood.
I had bluegrass playing on the radio.
Daddy said, "That picking and
grinnin' is the only way to go!"

I was all set and getting very excited about
the show I was about to bring.
My pal yelled, "On your marks, get set, GO!"
I thought, *Well, here goes nothing!*

I backed that truck right through the trees,
doing figure eights just for fun.
I hit a ramp and went airborne; the cats were on the run!

Limbs were cracking, tires squalling.
I hit every single jump.
I even parallel-parked that thing right
between a rock and a stump!

My buddy was shocked and amazed at this impossible task I had completed. He regretted this bet he had waged with me because he knew he had been defeated!

He shook my hand and congratulated
me on my reverse-driving skills,
And he jumped in shotgun beside me, and
we drove off for some major thrills!

About the Author

Brooke Whitfield, author of *Reverse Truck*, has always enjoyed writing, especially poems. She was inspired to write *Reverse Truck* after her nephew Garrett's favorite blue pickup truck really got stuck in reverse! Reverse Truck goes on many adventures in the stories she has written so far. Brooke is a twin, is married to Ben, and has her own set of twins, Ethan and Hannah, who keep her busy with their sports and hobbies. She has been a nurse for seventeen years.

CPSIA information can be obtained
at www.ICGtesting.com
Printed in the USA
BVHW061033291121
622781BV00010B/489